PIXAR

PIXAR

READY FOR ACTION!

A Collection of 5 Early Readers

Random House 🏠 New York

Random House and the colophon are registered trademarks of Penguin Random House LLC.

rhcbooks.com

ISBN 978-0-7364-4125-4

MANUFACTURED IN CHINA

10 9 8 7 6 5 4 3 2 1

Contents

BEST DAD
IN THE SEA

By Amy J. Tyler

Illustrated by the Disney Storybook Artists

Designed by Disney's Global Design Group

Random House 🏠 New York

Nemo loves his dad,
Marlin.

And Marlin loves Nemo.

But they are
very different.

Marlin is careful.

"Slow down, Nemo!"

Nemo is not.

"Come on, Dad!"

15

One day, Nemo is
TOO brave.

He swims far ahead.

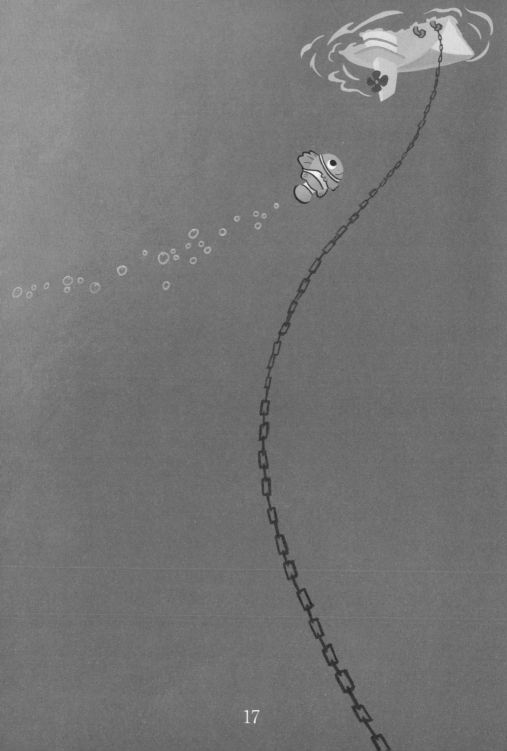

Oh, no! A diver.
Marlin cannot
see Nemo.

Nemo has been caught!

Marlin swims
after Nemo.

But he is too late.

PLOP!

Into a tank Nemo goes.

How will he
ever get home?

Marlin is sad.

He wants to search

for Nemo.

His friend Dory can help.

At first,
Marlin is very,
very afraid.

But not for long.

"My son needs me!"

Marlin says.

For Nemo,

Marlin is brave.

He is VERY brave!

Nemo hears
good news.

Help is on the way.

Nemo escapes!

Dory finds Nemo first.

They look for his dad.

They ask the crabs

for help.

They find Marlin.

But they get stuck

in a net.

Nemo has a plan.

"Swim down!" he says

to the fish.

They are free!

"You were so brave,"
says Nemo.

"You were brave, too,"
says his dad.

Nemo loves his dad.

And his dad loves him.

And they are not

so different after all!

Disney · PIXAR

THE GOOD DINOSAUR

The Journey Home

Disney · PIXAR

THE GOOD DINOSAUR

The Journey Home

By Bill Scollon

Illustrated by the Disney Storybook Art Team

Random House 🏠 New York

Arlo is a dinosaur.
He lives
with his family
on a farm.

Arlo is scared
of many things.
He is afraid
to leave the farm.

A wild boy steals food!

Arlo is scared.

He runs away.

Arlo and the boy
fall into the river.
The water sweeps
them away.

Arlo is far

from home.

The boy is gone.

Arlo is lost.

He is scared.

Arlo can follow the river

to get home.

The boy finds Arlo.

He brings food.

Arlo follows the boy

into the woods.

Arlo names the boy Spot.

They have fun together.

They become friends.

Arlo and Spot get lost.

They are attacked!

A pack of T. rexes
saves them.

Arlo and Spot are happy.

They will be home soon.

A human calls

to Spot.

Arlo is afraid that

Spot might leave.

But he stays with Arlo.

Arlo and Spot
are attacked again!
Spot is trapped
in a log.

This time,
Arlo is brave.
He fights
to help Spot.

A flash flood
is coming!
It almost carries
Spot away.

Arlo jumps
into the water.
He will save
his friend!

Arlo and Spot go
over a waterfall.
They swim to shore.
They are safe!

Spot meets a human family.
Arlo knows Spot should stay
with them.
Arlo and Spot say goodbye.

Arlo is a brave dinosaur.
He finds the farm
on his own.
Arlo is home!

By Liz Marsham

Illustrated by the Disney Storybook Art Team

Random House New York

A new racing season
is here!
Lightning McQueen
takes the lead.
His friends race hard.
They have fun, too.

Jackson Storm

is a new racer.

Lightning tries

to beat him.

Storm is too fast.

Lightning crashes!

Lightning watches a video
of his crew chief,
Doc Hudson.
Doc had a bad crash
and never raced again.
Lightning does not want
to stop racing.

A business car named Sterling

builds Lightning

a new training center.

Lightning is excited!

He is ready

to start training and racing.

Cruz Ramirez

is Lightning's new trainer.

She will use

the best training system

to make Lightning faster.

But the training system
is hard to use.
Lightning breaks it.

Lightning wants
to train his own way.
He takes Cruz
to the beach.

Cruz sinks

into the sand.

Lightning teaches her how

to race on the beach.

Lightning and Cruz

enter a small race.

They wear disguises.

They do not know the race

is the Thunder Hollow Crazy Eight!

Cars crash into each other.

A school bus named

Miss Fritter chases Cruz.

Lightning and Cruz want

to leave the race!

Lightning says

Cruz is not a real racer.

Cruz is sad.

She wants to leave.

Cruz has always wanted

to be a racer.

Lightning feels bad.

He takes her to

Doc Hudson's track.

Lightning and Cruz

meet some famous cars

who used to race with Doc.

They tell stories about him.

He once flipped

over another racer!

Lightning and Cruz train

with Doc's friends.

They pull heavy trailers.

Every day, they get

faster and stronger.

They have a lot of fun, too.

At the end of their training,

Cruz beats Lightning in a race.

She is faster!

Now it is time

for the big race in Florida.

Lightning is nervous.

Finally, the race begins!

Lightning thinks about Cruz.

Cruz did all the training,

just like Lightning.

Cruz is a great racer.

She just needs a chance.

Lightning goes to the pit.

He has an idea.

Cruz will finish the race!

Ramone paints Cruz.

Lightning will help her.

Cruz feels

excited and nervous.

She joins the race!

Cruz catches up to Storm.

Storm is a bad sport.

He pushes Cruz

into the wall.

Cruz remembers
one of Doc's tricks.
She flips over Storm
and wins the race!

Afterward,
Cruz quits her job
as a trainer.
Everyone is shocked!

Tex Dinoco will sponsor her.

She will be a racer!

Lightning will be

her crew chief.

Cruz and Lightning

get new paint jobs.

Lightning is happy

to race with his friend!

A Family Mystery

Adapted by Sarah Hernandez

Illustrated by the Disney Storybook Art Team

Random House 🏠 New York

Miguel Rivera lives in Mexico
with his big family.

Mamá Coco is

his great-grandmother.

Miguel loves her.

Before Miguel was born,
the Rivera home
was filled with music.
One day, Coco's papá left
to play music
all over the world.
He never came back.

Coco's mother is Mamá Imelda.
Imelda learned to make shoes
to help her family.
She has one rule:
NO MUSIC!

Miguel's abuelita

has the same rule.

But Miguel has a secret.

He does not want

to make shoes

like his family.

He loves music!

He sings and plays guitar

for his dog, Dante.

Ernesto de la Cruz is
Miguel's favorite musician.
Miguel knows all
his songs and movies.
He wants to be
just like Ernesto.

Miguel wants to play
in a talent show
on Día de los Muertos,
the Day of the Dead.
That is when family
in the Land of the Dead
visit the Land of the Living.

For Día de los Muertos,
the Riveras put photos
of their family
on an altar.

In a photo of Mamá Coco

when she was little,

her papá has a guitar.

It is Ernesto's!

Mamá Coco's papá is

Ernesto de la Cruz!

Abuelita says Miguel cannot

play in the talent show.

The family rule

is no music!

She smashes his guitar.

Miguel runs away.

He needs a new instrument.

He finds Ernesto's guitar

and plays it.

Suddenly,

Miguel can see

his family from

the Land of the Dead!

They are skeletons.

His family will take him
to Mamá Imelda.
Miguel needs a blessing
from a family member.
Then he can return
to the Land of the Living.

But Imelda's blessing
comes with
a condition:
no music.
Miguel runs off.

He meets Hector.

Hector knows Ernesto de la Cruz!

Miguel tells him Ernesto

is his only family member

and Miguel needs his blessing.

Hector will help Miguel

find Ernesto.

In return, Miguel will bring
Hector's photo to the
Land of the Living.
Hector paints Miguel
to look like a skeleton
so he will fit in.

Miguel enters a talent show.

Hector plays onstage with him.

The talent show host

says there is a family

looking for a live boy.

But Hector thought Ernesto
was Miguel's only family!
Miguel lied to him.
Miguel thinks Hector
will not help him find Ernesto.
He throws
Hector's photo at him.

Mamá Imelda finds Miguel.

She says he must choose

between family and music.

Miguel does not want to choose.

He storms off.

Miguel finds Ernesto

at his mansion.

Miguel plays a song.

Ernesto is happy to meet his

great-great-grandson!

Hector appears.

He and Ernesto used

to be friends.

But Hector is not happy

to see Ernesto.

Miguel finds out that Ernesto
stole Hector's songs
and his guitar!
Ernesto does not want
anyone to know.
He throws Hector and Miguel
into a pit!

If they are not rescued by sunrise,

Miguel will turn into a skeleton!

Hector used to write songs
for his daughter, Coco.
Mamá Coco is Hector's daughter!
Hector is Miguel's
great-great-grandfather!
If Coco does not remember Hector,
he will disappear.

Mamá Imelda saves
Hector and Miguel.
Everyone learns the truth
about Ernesto.

Hector and Imelda give Miguel
their blessing to go home.

Miguel sings Hector's song
to Mamá Coco.

The whole family watches.

She remembers Papá Hector!

Music fills their home

once again.

The Rivera family
love each other,
and they love music, too.
Music brings them
all together.

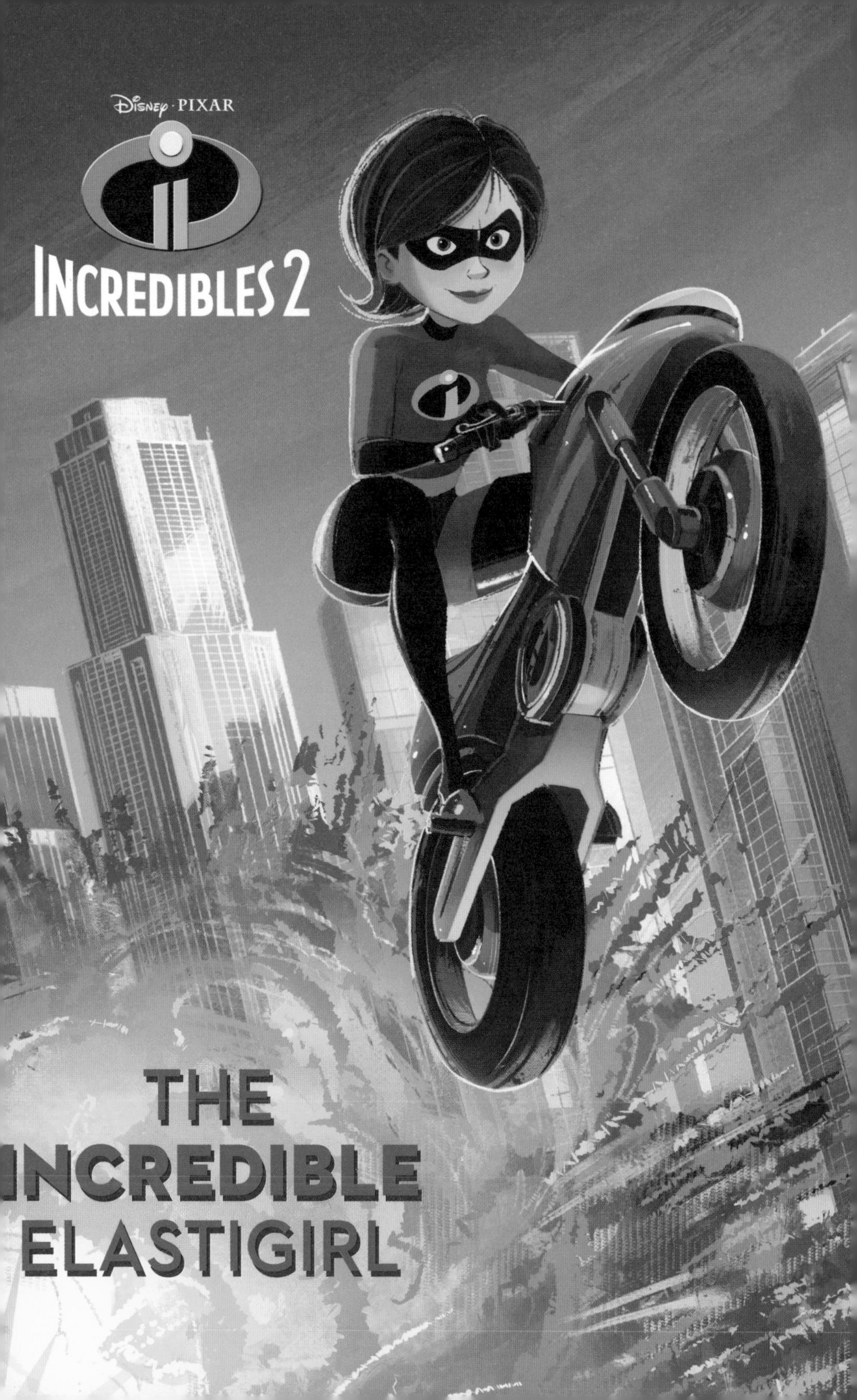
DISNEY · PIXAR
INCREDIBLES 2
THE INCREDIBLE ELASTIGIRL

Disney · PIXAR

INCREDIBLES 2

THE
INCREDIBLE
ELASTIGIRL

By Natasha Bouchard

Illustrated by the Disney Storybook Art Team

Random House 🏠 New York

Helen Parr is a Super
called Elastigirl.
She can stretch, bend, and twist
into any shape.
Her husband
is Mr. Incredible.
He is a Super, too.

With their family,
they battle
the Underminer,
an evil villain.
The Underminer tries
to destroy the city.

The Underminer steals money
from the banks.
The Supers try to stop him,
but he gets away.

The Underminer

has left a big mess.

The city is ruined!

Everyone blames the Supers.

The Supers' agency
is shut down.
Supers are illegal.
The Parr family must find
a new place to live.

Winston Deavor is a rich man.

He wants to help Mr. Incredible,

Elastigirl, and their friend Frozone.

He wants to show the public

that the city needs Supers.

His sister, Evelyn, built
a special camera
for the Supersuits.
It will film the Supers
in action.

Winston lets the Parr family live
in one of his many homes.
The huge house is full
of waterfalls and pools!

Elastigirl gets the first job.

She puts on her new Supersuit.

She gets on her bike.

Mr. Incredible will stay home
with Jack-Jack, Violet,
and Dash.

Elastigirl speeds after
a runaway train.
She must save the train
before it crashes.

Elastigirl stops the train
just in time!
The villain Screenslaver
wanted it to crash.

Elastigirl is a hero
for saving the train.
She is excited!
She tells Mr. Incredible
about her mission.

Mr. Incredible watches Elastigirl

on every news channel.

The public loves her!

The Screenslaver

has captured

an important ambassador!

Elastigirl leaps to a helicopter.

She saves the ambassador!

Elastigirl uses a special device

to track down the Screenslaver.

She blows up

like a parachute.

She catches the villain!

But something
does not feel right.
Elastigirl checks the camera
on her suit.
She zooms in.

Evelyn is worried.

Elastigirl has seen too much.

Evelyn is the Screenslaver!

She hypnotizes Elastigirl

with her hypno-goggles.

Evelyn is working

against the Supers.

Elastigirl tries
to break free,
but she cannot move.

Meanwhile,
Winston's plan
is working.
World leaders
make Supers legal again.

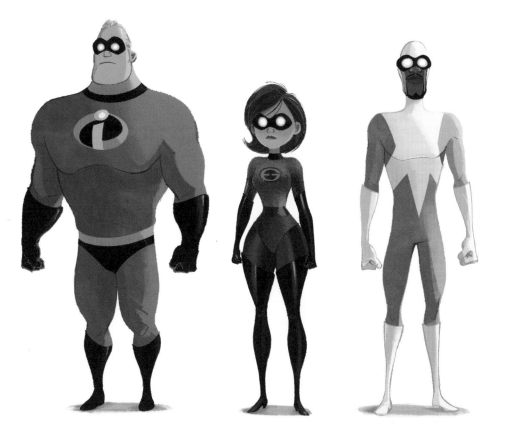

Evelyn wants to stop them.

She tricks Mr. Incredible.

She hypnotizes him
and Frozone, too.

Just then,

Violet, Dash,

and Jack-Jack arrive!

Jack-Jack pulls the hypno-goggles

off Elastigirl.

Elastigirl fights Evelyn.

Elastigirl stops Evelyn!

The police arrest her.

The Supers save the city

and become legal again!

Thanks to Elastigirl,

Supers will keep the city safe!